The Curious Wonderful Adventures of Charlie

by Dr. C. Wheatcroft.

Chapter 1

Charlie was a child just like any other

With a mum, a dad, 2 sisters and 1 brother

They lived in an

upstairs

downstairs

house

But one day something make it all change

A gift he was given that

happened that would

would make his life strange

A peculiar object

a most curious thing

A corduroy wetsuit

not the crown of a king

And
when

he wore
it

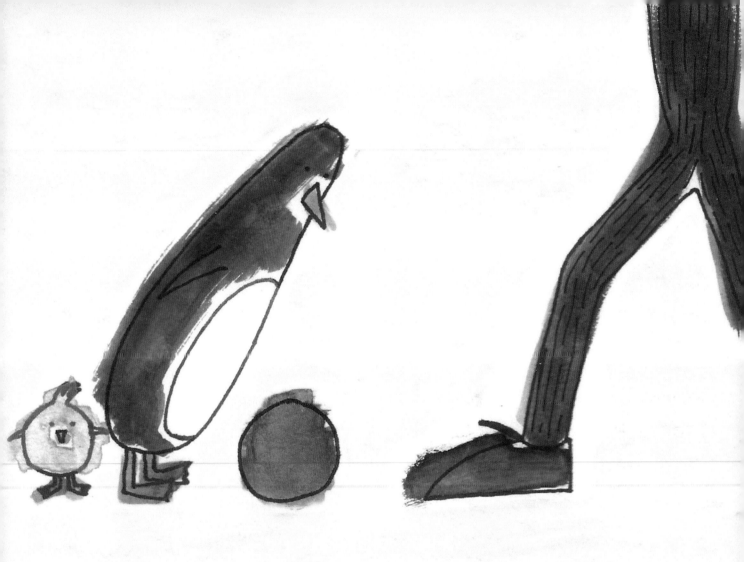

His mind would wander
his imagination soar

With hardly time to even leave his front door

The places he'd go and the
things he'd see

The world's
spottiest toad

and its tallest tree

He'd live out

and realise things aren't

wonderful dreams

always as they seem

But no one would believe

So he came up with a plan that

would make them believe

But what could this bright idea be?

Well, of course

he would find a kiwi

He'd search far and wide

under hill and beyond the tide

And he'd bring that bird back home again

So the truth of his stories would be plain

And now
we'll
discover

And followed Charlie on his quest

Then it danced and jived

This adventure
like
no other

A journey
to

faraway
lands

Chapter 2

To sunburnt Australia
where kangaroos roam

A Land down under

with a ridiculous number

Of animals

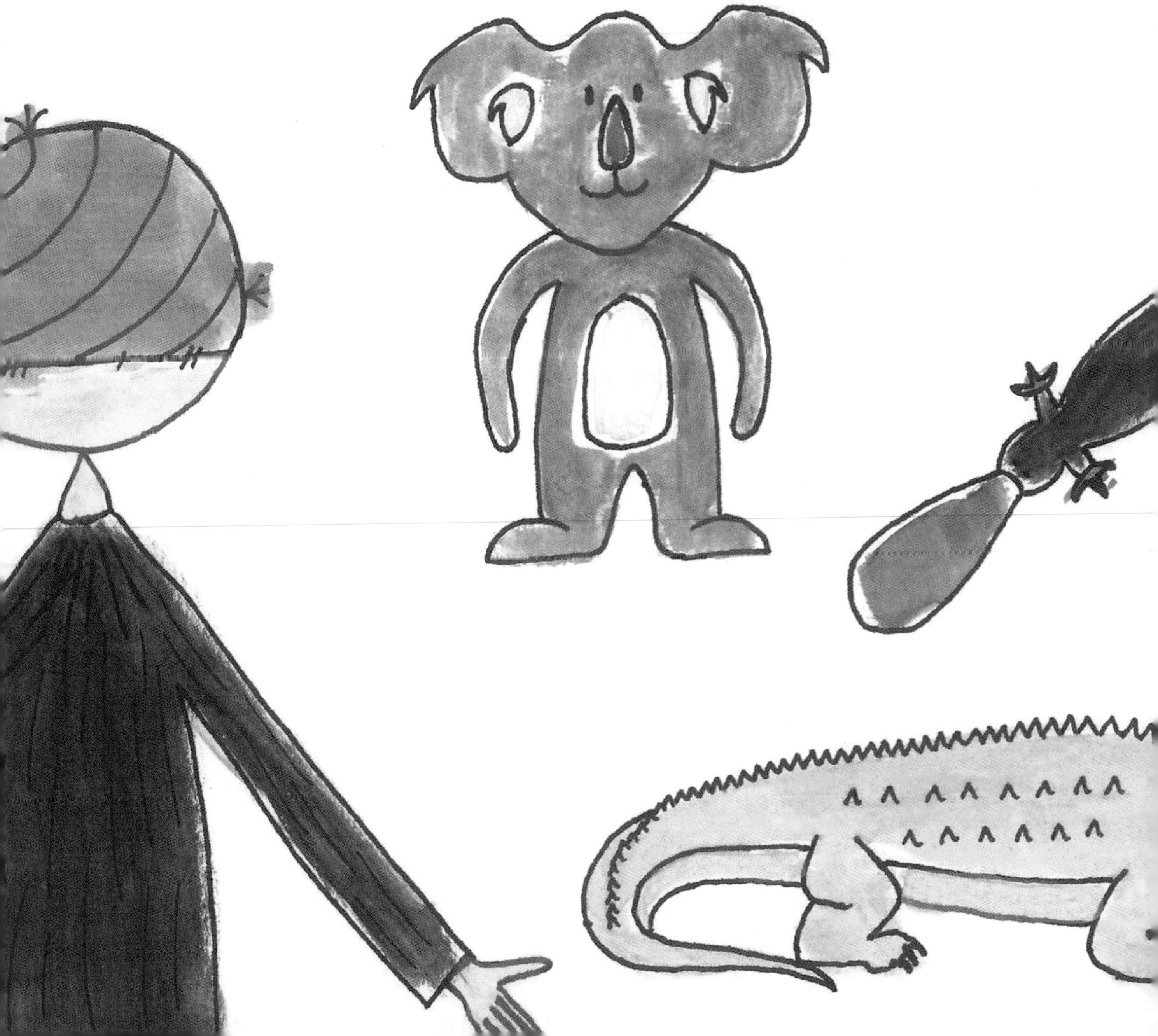

The home of the platypus

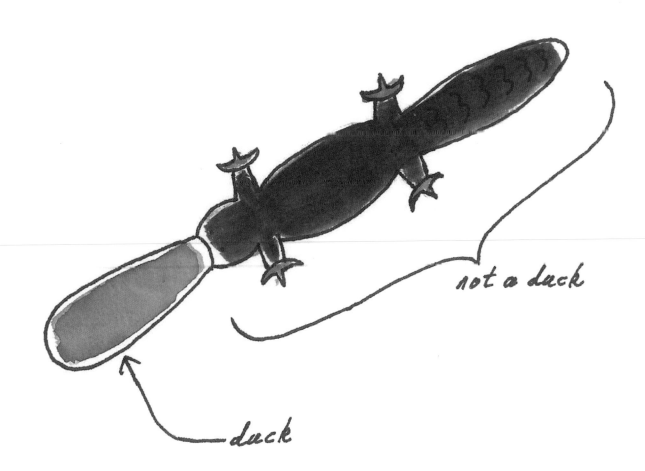

not a duck

duck

And miles of unspoilt bush

He walked over red desert flats

Past men with corks

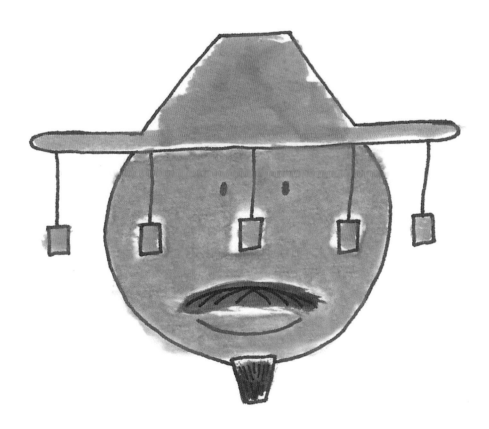

on their hats

he spot a kiwi
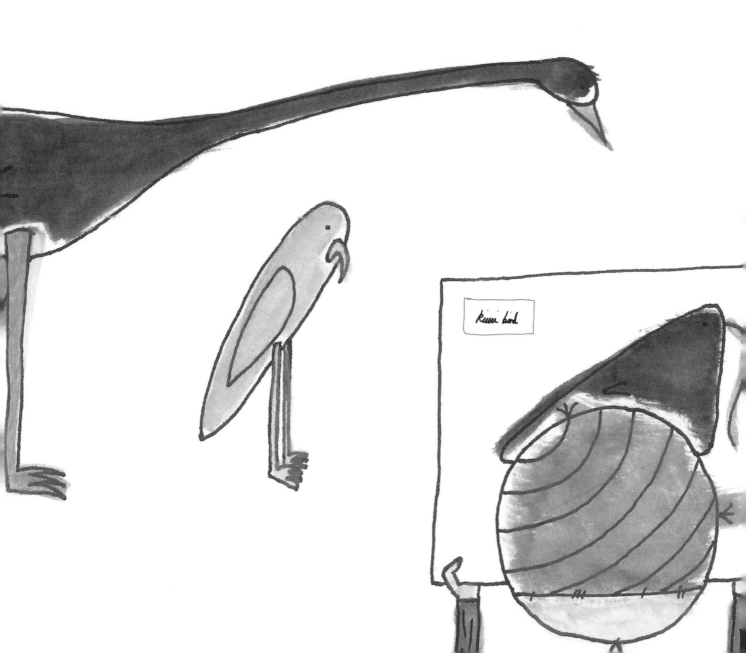

Finally he decided

That he'd been misguided

And would search in another place

So past emu and crocodile he raced

Until reaching

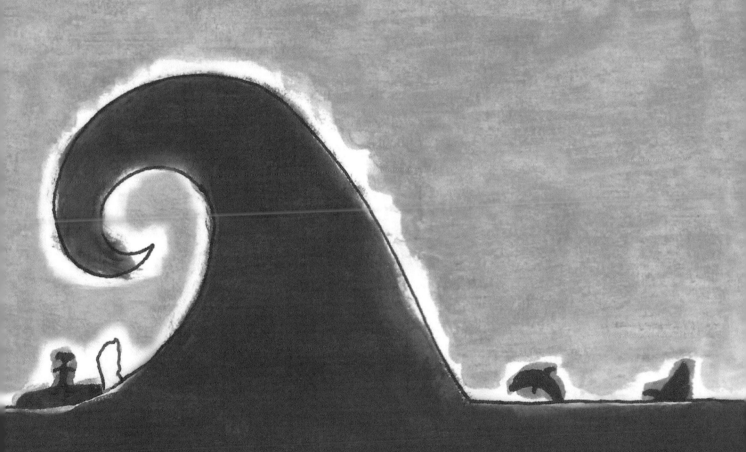

the sapphire sea

Where koala bears surf

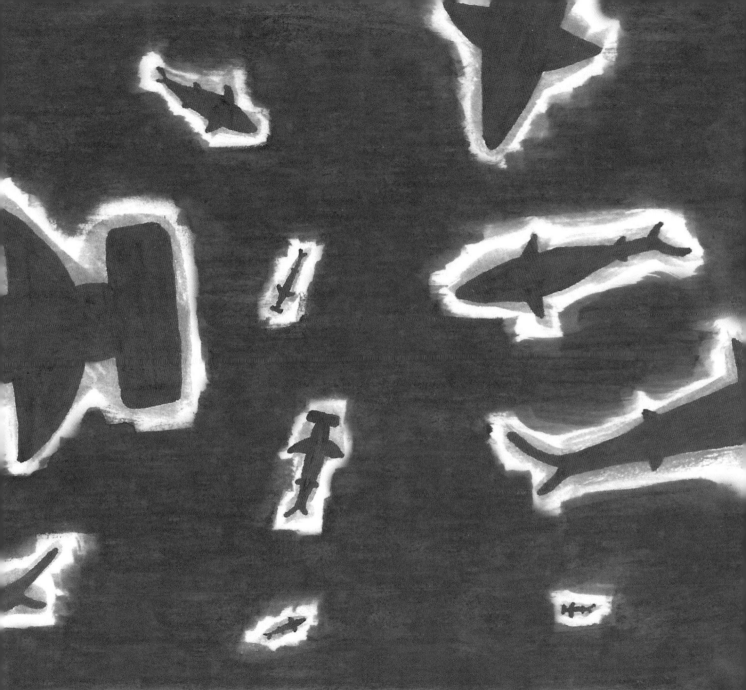

And the sharks have their turf

Having not learnt how to sail

And continued on

free as can be

And sleeping under a giant leaf

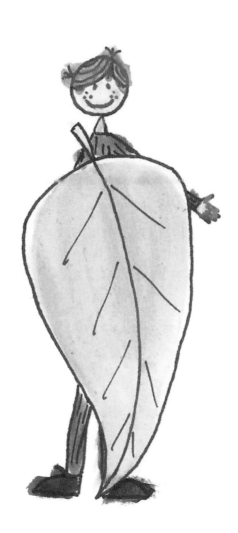

ALL the while dreaming
of a land tall and proud

Aotearoa, the land
of the long white cloud

Maybe there he'd

find what he seeked

Chapter 3

To Aotearoa where the earth meets the sky

And the wandering albatross
ever does fly

Though that land isn't ruled

But the tiniest creature

by the big or the strong

with the loveliest song

The piwakawaka the bravest of birds

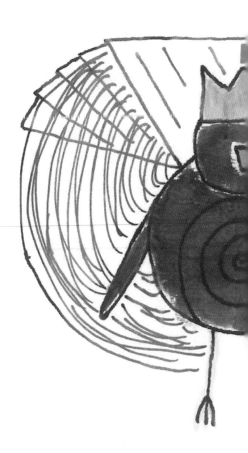

With its fanshaped tail
so quick that it's blurred

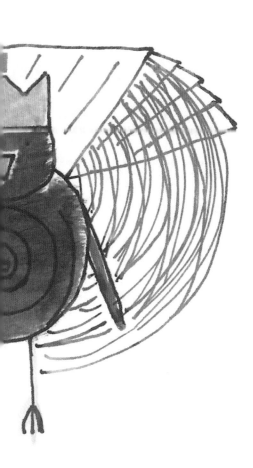

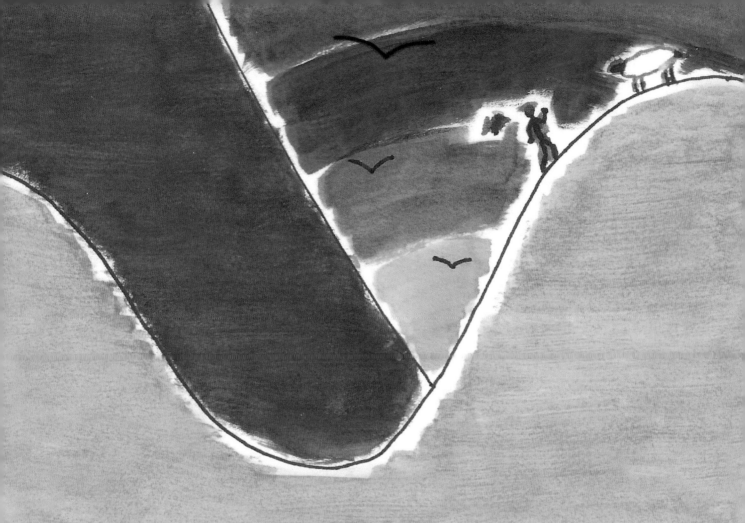

As onward through that land
he pressed

Over mightiest mountain
atop which he stood

And then down again
into magical wood

Then from the corner
of one careful eye

What did Charlie manage to spy?

A kiwibird and no mistake

With its nose
as long and thin as a rake

So he told of the
corduroy wetsuit

And the journey he'd made so far

That his stories were under dispute

Mr kiwi said in return

So they walked back through the
returned to

And a final goodbye to that
wondrous world

first to see the new day dawn,
first to wave the sun goodbye,

land and at last
the sea

Aotearoa,

East
of the
sea

and South of the sun

and welcome in each morn,
and say hello to starlit sky

Charlie smiled as he began his reply

But his friends all began to laugh at Charlie

Until out from behind him walked

Mr Kiwi

But said

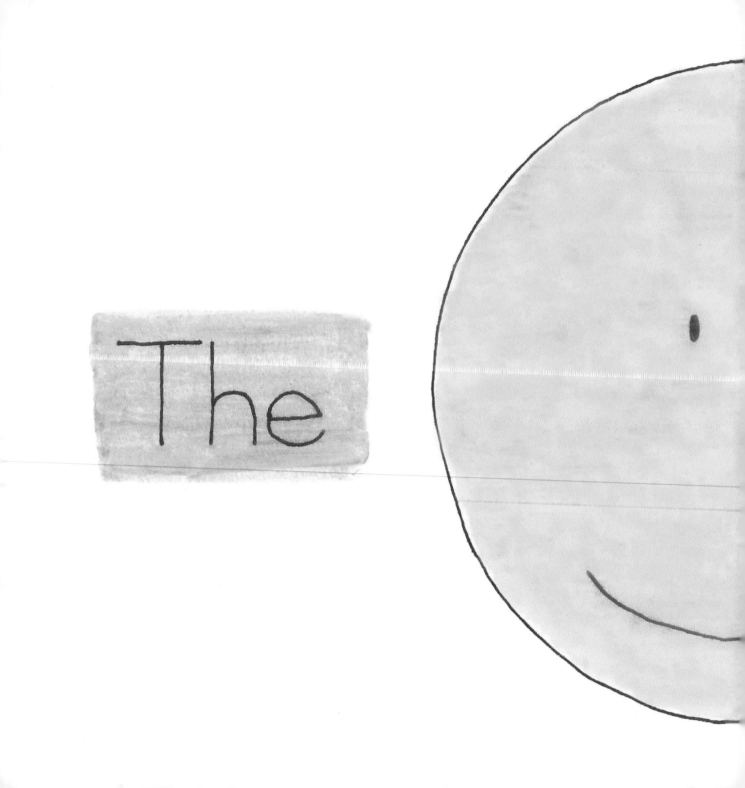

The

End

Printed in Great Britain
by Amazon